FLAME RIDERS BOOK 1

BORN OF FIRE

C.A. VARIAN

Copyright © 2023 by C.A. Varian

All rights reserved.

No part of this publication may be reproduced, distributed, or transmitted in any form or by any means, including photocopying, recording, or other electronic or mechanical methods, without the prior written permission of the publisher, except as permitted by U.S. copyright law. For permission requests, contact C.A. Varian.

The story, all names, characters, and incidents portrayed in this production are fictitious. No identification with actual persons (living or deceased), places, buildings, and products is intended or should be inferred.

Book Cover by Leigh Cover Designs

Formatting by Me!

1st edition 2023

Contents

Dedication		V
		VII
1.	Dreaming of Adventure	3
2.	Beyond the Mountains	11
3.	Only Dreams	19
4.	Dire Situation	29
5.	Under the Stars	37
6.	Dangers of the Forest	45
7.	Ancient Embrace	53
8.	Run!	63
9.	Ancient Arms	71
10.	Thrill of Discovery	77
11.	Precious Cargo	85
12.	The Hiding Spot	95

13.	The Secret	103
14.	Early Riser	109
15.	The Bond	115
16.	Miracle in the Ashes	123
17.	The Flame Riders	131
Also By		137
About the Author		139

This book is dedicated to my former student, Joshua, and all the other amazing kids I've taught over my twelve years as a public school teacher. Y'all begged me to write a kid's story, so I hope I did it justice.

I miss and love you all, so find me on social media and update me on your life!

Love, Mrs. V

Chapter 1

Dreaming of Adventure

The sun bathed fifteen-year-old Josu Greensword's family farm in Eldoria with a warm, golden glow. Lush green fields stretched as far as the eye can see, dotted with the farm's animals grazing on vibrant grass. The cozy farmhouse, with its sloping roof and whitewashed walls, nestled among the rolling hills like a permanent fixture, a beacon of love and security in the vast countryside.

"Josu! Hurry up, little brother!" Rennan Greensword called out, ruffling Josu's short, brown hair as he caught up.

Furrowing his brow, Josu batted his brother's hand away. "Hey!" Even as he fussed, his bright blue eyes sparkled with mischief. "I'm not that little anymore!"

"Sure, you're not." Rennan grinned. "But you've still got a lot to learn."

Although Josu rolled his eyes, he couldn't help a small smile from creeping onto his face. He knew Rennan was right, and he was eager to soak up all the knowledge and skills he could from his older brother. There was just something about the way Rennan carried himself with a confidence and strength that Josu admired.

"Alright, so what's the plan for today?" Josu asked, shifting his weight between his feet, itching to get started on their training session.

"Patience, young grasshopper," Rennan said with mock seriousness. "Today, we'll be focusing on your swordsmanship. Remember, it's not just about brute force. You need to be strategic and quick."

Taking in every word as if it were gospel, Josu nodded. "Got it. Strategic and quick."

"Wait." Even as Rennan pulled out the practice swords, Josu's gaze drifted toward the distant Elder Mountains. "What lies beyond those peaks, Rennan?"

"Josu, focus." Rennan's voice snapped him back to reality. "You'll have plenty of time to daydream after we're done."

"Sorry." Turning his attention back to his brother, Josu shook his head to clear the lingering thoughts of adventure and mystery that always clouded his mind.

"Alright. Let's get started." Turning around, Rennan tossed Josu a wooden sword.

Still, even as they sparred, Josu's mind couldn't help but wander again, filling with images of daring quests and legendary battles. He knew he needed to concentrate on the task at hand, but the call of adventure was impossible to ignore.

"Pay attention, Josu!" Rennan shouted, breaking through his reverie once more. "If you're not going to take this seriously, I don't know why we're wasting our time out here."

"Sorry, Rennan." A twinge of guilt filled Josu's chest. He appreciated his brother teaching him, but he just yearned to be brave and explore his world. "I promise I'll do better."

Rennan's eyes softened, understanding on his face. "Good. Now, let's try that last move again. And this time, keep your mind on what you're doing."

As they continued to train, Josu made a conscious effort to stay focused, but his heart still longed for the thrilling unknown that lay just beyond the horizon. He knew that one day, he would find his own adventure, and when that day came, he would be ready.

The late afternoon sun warmed the air as Josu and his father, Erno, trudged through the vibrant green fields of their family farm, his morning training session long over. Their boots squelched in the damp earth, leaving a trail of muddy footprints behind them. "These crops are looking good." Bending down, Erno examined a row of ripe squash. "Thanks to your hard work, son," he continued, clapping Josu on the back with a proud grin. Josu's heart squeezed as he gazed at the fruits of their labor, feeling a sense of accomplishment well up inside him. "Alright. Let's start by feeding the animals before it gets too dark."

Eager to continue helping his father with their daily chores, Josu nodded. "Yes, sir."

As they moved from the fields to the barn, the grunts and snuffles of the pigs and the gentle lowing of the cows filled the chilly air. The smell of hay and manure mingled with the crisp autumn breeze brought a smile to Josu's face.

"Remember, Josu," Erno called over the noise of the animals, "a well-fed animal is a happy animal, and a happy animal makes for a healthy farm."

"Got it, Dad!" Josu shouted back, scooping a generous portion of feed into each trough. He marveled at his father's ability to know exactly what needed to be done when and how, as if he could read the land itself.

"Josu, my boy, do you know why we work so hard every day?" Erno asked as they finished tending to the last of the animals, his warm hazel eyes meeting Josu's gaze.

Josu thought for a moment, feeling the weight of responsibility settle on his young shoulders. "Is it because we need to provide for our family?"

"Exactly." A proud smile spread across Erno's face. "Without our hard work and perseverance, we wouldn't be able to put food on the table or care for the land that has been in our family for generations."

"Sometimes I wish I could go on adventures like the heroes in the stories," Josu confessed, his voice tinged with longing. "But I know our family needs me here."

Taking a step closer, Erno placed a hand on his son's shoulder. "Josu, you have a strong heart and a curious mind. Your dedication to our family and our farm is truly commendable. Who knows, maybe one day you'll find adventure right here at home."

Chapter 2

Beyond the Mountains

After completing the day's chores, Josu ambled to the farm's edge, where Rennan was gearing up for their evening combat training. His brother was in the Eldorian military and made frequent trips to the capital to sell the farm's crops at the market, so Josu loved spending time with him when he was home.

Approaching, Josu caught Rennan's eye, eliciting a smile. "Ah, there you are, little brother! I thought you'd decided to run away and join the heroes from your stories."

Josu grinned, delivering a playful punch to his brother's arm. "Not today. But I'm ready to give you a run for your money in our training."

"Is that so?" Rennan raised an eyebrow, a mischievous sparkle in his intense blue eyes. "Well then, let's see what you've got then! I bet I can still whip you!"

The resonant clack of wooden swords echoed across the silent fields as the two brothers sparred. Even though he was still learning, Josu matched Rennan's graceful steps, anticipating his moves as he'd done countless times before.

"Remember, Josu, keep your guard up." Lifting his arm, Rennan blocked a swift strike from his younger brother, spinning around and swiping low. "If this were a real battle, one lapse could be the end of you."

"I know." Josu panted, sweat dripping down his brow. He couldn't help but admire Rennan's skill, wondering if he would ever be as proficient in combat. "But when will I ever need these skills? We're just simple farmers."

Lowering his weapon, Rennan crouched down until he was at Josu's eye level. "True, but we have a duty to protect our family and our land. You never know when danger might come knocking at our door. You also never know if the king will summon you to his guard just like he did to me."

Although Josu nodded, the weight of his brother's words sent a chill down his spine. He knew his older brother was right. Embracing the responsibility to protect his home only intensified his gratitude for learning valuable skills from Rennan.

Smiling, Rennan patted Josu on the back. "Alright. Let's try archery next."

They left their practice swords behind and strolled toward their archery targets, their boots crunching on the gravel path leading to the farmhouse. The tranquil sounds of songbirds filled the air, and the scent of freshly tilled earth mingled with the fragrant blossoms of pear trees lining the fields, creating a soothing atmosphere. This allowed Josu to lose himself in thought as they practiced their aim with bows and arrows. With each arrow released, he envisioned the thrill of venturing beyond the farm, facing unknown dangers, and protecting those he loved. Gratitude for Rennan's guidance filled his heart. His brother's expertise as an experienced hunter proved invaluable, and Josu eagerly anticipated the day when he would join Rennan on a hunt, facing the wild with courage. Until then, he would practice his aim and hone his skills, improving every day.

When Josu's next shot found its mark, Rennan clapped. "Good shot! You're keep getting better, little brother."

"Thanks to you." A smile spread across Josu's face at his brother's praise. "I'm lucky to have you as my teacher."

With a smile, Rennan handed Josu another arrow. "No need to be so humble, Josu. You've worked hard, and you deserve the recognition."

"Thanks." Feeling more confident than ever, he notched the arrow and took aim. When he released it, it flew straight and true, hitting the center of the target.

"Remember," Rennan said, placing a hand on Josu's shoulder. "Your greatest strength lies not just in your skills, but in your heart. Never forget how much our family means to us, and what we would do to protect it."

Hearing his brother's words, Josu felt renewed determination to be the best version of himself—for his family, for their land, and for the adventures he was sure to face someday.

Approaching the house when their training finished, the warm aroma of baking bread filled the air, making Josu's stomach rumble. His gaze drifted toward the distant Elder Mountains, whose majestic peaks were bathed in the brilliant hues of the setting sun.

"Rennan..." Stopping on his path, Josu hesitated. "What do you really think lies beyond those mountains? Surely there must be more to the world than just our farm and the kingdom?"

Rennan looked thoughtful for a moment before responding. "There are vast kingdoms, enchanted forests, and ancient ruins hidden deep within and past those mountains, but you have to be brave to venture far enough to see them and learn their secrets. Perhaps one day, we'll explore those lands ourselves." Rennan smiled, his eyes twinkling. "We'll need courage, determination, and a bit of luck, but I'm sure the journey will be worth it when we take it."

"Really?" Josu's eyes widened, his imagination soaring as he pictured himself and Rennan, sword and bow in hand, traversing treacherous paths and uncovering long-lost secrets. He imagined himself becoming a great adventurer, roaming the world and discovering new places.

"Perhaps." Reaching out, Rennan ruffled his little brother's hair again. "But for now, let's focus on what's right in front of us. Remember, our family depends on us to keep this farm thriving, and it's our duty to tend to it."

Taking one more glance at the mountains, Josu nodded. "Alright. But one day, Rennan, we'll see what lies beyond those peaks. I just have to."

Chapter 3
Only Dreams

The early morning sun was rising in the sky, telling the roosters it's time to crow for a new day. With them alerting their flock of the time, Josu approached the small wooden fence separating their property from the vast Eldorian landscape. Leaning against the fence, he gazed into the distance, watching the animals grazing in the field.

"Josu!" called out a spirited voice from behind him. Turning around, his heart pounded when he saw Aelara Windwhisper bounding toward him, her flowing red hair trailing behind her like a fiery comet. Her sharp green eyes sparkled with excitement as she stood beside him at the fence, bringing a genuine grin to his face.

"Morning, Aelara."

"Did you finish your chores already?" Resting her elbows on the fence, Aelara gazed out at the sprawling countryside.

"Not yet." Josu kicked at the dirt beneath his feet. "My dad and I have a few more things to do, but I wanted to take a break for a moment to catch my breath."

Aelara nodded. For a moment, they stood in silence, watching as the sun rose and painted the world around them in brilliant shades of orange, pink, and gold.

"Sometimes," Josu began, his voice barely above a whisper, "I wish we could leave this place. Go on an adventure, explore the world... Do something other than plow fields and tend to animals."

Aelara's eyes sparkled with shared yearning. "Wouldn't that be something? Imagine traveling through forests and climbing mountains, sailing across oceans, and discovering unknown places."

Although Josu knew that such dreams were only dreams, he still smiled. He couldn't abandon his family for a life of adventure because they depended on him. In spite of that, he found comfort in knowing that Aelara understood his feelings.

With a stunning smile on her face, Aelara turned to him. "We're still young. One day, we'll be able to fulfill those dreams. You're smart, Josu. If anyone can provide for their family while still exploring the world, you can."

While Josu finished helping his father with their chores, Aelara went inside and assisted his mother in the kitchen. When he was done, he asked his father to see his map of the continent, an old map he'd found in a box in the attic long ago, taking it outside.

Sitting cross-legged on the grassy hill, he traced the uneven edges of the torn map. Aelara sat next to him, her long red hair dancing in the breeze like a wild flame. She studied the map with an intensity that made Josu's heart race. Despite never telling her, he thought Aelara was the most beautiful girl in the world.

"Is this what your father found in the attic?" Aelara asked, her voice barely audible above the rustling leaves.

"Yep! He said he no longer needed it, so I could have it."

Reaching forward, Aelara traced a path across the map, pointing at a cluster of islands labeled 'The Veiled Archipelago.' "Look at all these places we've never heard of. Imagine the secrets hidden there."

"Or the treasures!" Josu chimed in, unable to contain his excitement. Imagining what adventures might await them, his eyes sparkled with curiosity.

"Ha! You and your treasures." Giggling, Aelara nudged him with her shoulder. "You know, not every adventure has to end with us finding a chest full of gold."

"Of course not, but it certainly wouldn't hurt, would it?" A warmth spread in Josu's chest, a feeling he only experienced when he was with Aelara.

"Seriously, though," she said, turning to face him, her eyes alight. "I want to explore everything, Josu—every last corner of this world. Learn its secrets and see its wonders. Don't you?"

"More than anything." The sun shined bright as Josu gazed at the horizon, making the surface of the pond sparkle like diamonds. "But we can't just leave our families behind."

"Maybe we don't have to," Aelara mused, her eyes still on the map. "Maybe we can find a way to bring them along, or at least make sure they're taking care of while we're gone."

Hope kindled in Josu's chest at the thought. "Really? You think we could do that?"

"Of course!" Aelara said, rising to her knees. "We just have to be clever, resourceful, and—"

Grinning wider, she flicked a strand of her hair over her shoulder. "—perhaps a bit daring."

Josu laughed, feeling the weight of his responsibilities ease ever so slightly. "I'm definitely daring, Aelara."

"Tell me, Josu," Aelara said, her voice barely above a whisper as they huddled close, their fingers tracing the inked lines of the map spread out before them. "Which place would you visit first?"

Josu scanned the parchment, taking in the names that dotted the landscape like stars in the night sky. "There's a city to the east," he began, his voice hesitant but growing steadier with each word. "It's called Veridia. They say the streets are paved with emerald stones, and the market is filled with treasures from all corners of the world."

"Veridia." Leaning in closer, Aelera's eyes lit up brighter. "I've heard stories about it too. They say the people there can talk to animals, and the royal gardens are filled with flowers that never wilt."

"Imagine what we could learn there," Josu mused, his heart racing at the thought of exploring the fabled city with Aelara by his side. "We could discover new ways to farm, or find rare seeds that would make our crops flourish."

Aelara nodded, her eyes already darting to another location on the map. "And after Veridia, we could journey to the Silver Peak Mountains. Legend says there are ancient caves hidden there, guarded by creatures with scales as hard as steel."

"Dragons!" Josu blurted out, a thrill rippling through him at the mere mention of the mythical beasts. "I've always wanted to see one up close, but dad says they've gone extinct."

Aelara frowned, plopping back on the ground beside him. "Well... we should still search for them—just in case!"

Josu grinned, his mind filling with images of soaring through the air on the back of a dragon, and Aelara beside him, her hair streaming in the wind like a fiery banner as they touched the clouds. "If we did find a dragon, we'd be unstoppable. Just think of the adventures we'd have! We would be able to go anywhere!"

The more they spoke about their dreams of visiting distant lands and encountering mythical creatures, the more excited Josu became, his chest filling with warmth that threatened to burst. For the first time in his life, he dared to imagine a world beyond the confines of the farm—a world filled with discovery and wonder.

Chapter 4

Dire Situation

Later that day, as the sun set again on the farm, chickens pecked at the ground near the weathered barn, which had seen better days. The fields of wheat and corn swayed gently in the breeze, their once vibrant colors now faded with the passing of harvest season. The paint on its walls chipped, and the roof sagged beneath neglect and time. A place that once thrived was now teetering on the brink of ruin.

At the edge of one field, Josu stood, taking in the landscape, his sadness and determination battling in his chest. Although he knew his family struggled to make ends meet, he couldn't bear to see his parents work to the bone just to stay afloat. Wishing he could help, he scuffed his shoes in the dirt, sending a small cloud of dust up into the air.

"Hey, kiddo," his father called, wiping sweat from his brow as he trudged through the field toward him. "Whatcha doing?"

Turning to his father, Josu tried to put on a happier face. "Just thinking about ways to improve things around here."

His father sighed and looked around at their modest farm. "I know it's tough, son, but we're doing the best we can."

"There must be something I can do." His voice filled with conviction as his hands clenched into fists at his sides. "I am not going to stand by and watch our farm fall apart!"

Taking a step toward Josu, his father pressed a calloused hand against his shoulder. "Josu, you are already helping plenty, but I appreciate your willingness to help more."

"Please, Dad," Josu pleaded. "There must be something out there that can turn our luck around. I can do more for our family. Rennan was already serving when he wasn't much older than I am now."

Pride filled his father's eyes as he looked at him. "Alright, Josu," he relented, a small smile appearing on his tired face. "I will not stand in your way if you can find a way to help. Just promise me you will be careful, okay? At the end of the day, you're needed here."

"Of course, Dad! I promise!" Hope expanded in Josu's chest, his mind already whirring with ideas as he plotted his course of action. To resolve his family's problems, he would do whatever it took. It was important to him to make his family proud.

Standing in front of the stove, his mother turned to smile at him as she stirred whatever was cooking in the pot. "Are you ready for dinner?"

"Almost!" With his mind still racing with ideas about how he could help save their farm, he couldn't have dinner just yet, not when there was work to be done.

As he was leaving the kitchen, his father entered the room, looking weary from another long workday.

"We've got to find a way," his father muttered under his breath, unaware that Josu was listening.

Glancing over at her husband, his mother's brow furrowed. In a hushed voice, she asked, "Are we really in this much trouble?"

Erno nodded, rubbing the back of his neck. "Things are bad, Lila. The crops aren't growing like they used to, and we barely make enough to cover our debts."

Listening to his parents' conversation from the hall, Josu's heart clenched at their despair. In order to save the situation, something needed to be done as soon as possible. In the midst of his racing thoughts, he suddenly had an idea—one that might just change everything.

"Mom, Dad," Josu interjected, stepping out of his hiding spot. "What if I told you there might be a way out of this?"

His parents looked at him, their faces filled with surprise. "What do you mean, Josu?" his mother asked, her eyes flicking to her husband.

Excitement sending his heart into a frantic beat. "Have you ever been mining in the Elder Mountains? They say the mountains are full of gemstones, just waiting to be discovered!"

"Josu, those mountains are dangerous," his father said, his face clouding with concern. "And it's more than a day's hike from here. It's not the same as going to town."

"But think about it, Dad! If I could find just a few gemstones, we could sell them and save the farm! It's worth a try, isn't it?"

In the midst of their dire situation, Josu's parents exchanged glances, the expression on their faces showing how torn they were between wanting to protect their son and needing a solution.

"Is this really what you want to do, Josu?" his mother asked, her voice wavering. "I know you're capable, but it's a huge risk."

"Mom, I have to do something." Even as anxiety buzzed beneath his skin, Josu straightened his spine. "I can't just sit here while our family struggles. I'll be careful. I promise!"

After studying his son's face for a moment, Erno nodded. "Okay, son, but you must take all the necessary precautions. You can't go alone and not for longer than three days. After that, I will be forced to leave my work here at the farm and go look for you. And if you think it's too dangerous, you must return home immediately. Understood?"

Josu nodded, his heart thumping with excitement. "I understand!"

Chapter 5

Under the Stars

While Josu meticulously folded his clothes and placed them into his leather backpack, Aelara carefully arranged her quiver of arrows. The two friends were about to embark on a thrilling journey to the Elder Mountains, following a map they found in Josu's parents' bedroom. In addition to food rations, camping essentials, and weapons, they double-checked their supplies, including Josu's sword and Aelara's polished longbow.

Josu's body buzzed with excitement as he asked, "Are we forgetting anything?"

"Josu, you've checked that list at least three times now." Aelara rolled her eyes. "We're prepared. Let's go."

With their gear in hand, they bid farewell to Josu's parents, stopping at Aelara's house down the road to check in with her father one more time before they left the comforts of their village and plunged into the wilderness.

In the shadow of the leafy canopy above, the sun filtered through to illuminate the forest floor, creating shifting patterns of light and shadow. Inhaling deeply, Josu's senses were overwhelmed by the intoxicating aroma of damp soil and pine, the adrenaline inside him surging like a wildfire. Their footsteps were accompanied by the sounds of the forest—birdsong echoing through the trees and distant animal calls. The crunching of leaves beneath their feet provided a rhythm Josu found oddly comforting.

As they ventured deeper into the woods, Aelara held her dagger at the ready, walking beside Josu, leaves crunching beneath their feet. "Keep your wits about you. The Elder Mountains are full of mystery, and not all of it is friendly."

Despite his confidence that they were safe, Josu tightened the grip on his sword, his chest squeezing uncomfortably as the shadows seemed to close in around them. "Together we'll be more than a match for anything, Aelara. Don't worry."

Aelara nodded, her sharp green eyes scanning their surroundings.

The tension in the air was palpable, and Josu knew Aelara felt it as well. Taking a deep breath to calm his nerves, he reminded himself that he had to be brave for them both. With his obligations to the kingdom's military ranks, and his trips to the capital's market to sell the crops from their farm, Rennan could not go in Josu's stead. Their parents were depending on him, as was Aelara's father. Both of their families needed a lucky find.

"Did you ever think we'd be traveling this far from home, Aelara?" he asked, attempting to redirect their attention.

Shaking her head, she flashed him a crooked smile. "Never. But after dreaming about exploring beyond our little village, this was exactly the kind of adventure I hoped for."

Josu smiled, his heart swelling with admiration for his fearless friend. It was true that she had always been the more daring of the two, often leading them into mischief, like the time they chased a cat up a tree and couldn't get back down.

"Is it strange I'm missing my family already?" he asked, an ache tightening his chest.

"Of course not." Aelara's smile faltered, her own homesickness playing across her features. "They're your family. It's only natural to miss them. I miss my dad too. Ever since we lost my mom, he's worked so hard to take care of me and our farm. I know he was nervous to let me go, but both of our families need help, and just think of the stories we'll have to tell them when we return. Plus, they trusted us to make this journey, so we don't want to disappoint them."

"True." Josu was somewhat comforted by her words. "And I'm sure they'll be proud of us when we return victorious. Boys my age are already serving in the king's guard. Rennan joined the military when he wasn't much older than I am now."

The sun descended as the day wore on, gradually replacing its warm hues with cool, dusky ones. Recognizing they would need a place to camp for the night, Josu scanned the area until he found a small clearing off the main path.

"Over there." He pointed, sliding his sword into its sheath. As a team, they moved into the open area, quickly getting their equipment sorted out and setting up for an overnight stay.

While Josu gathered sticks and branches to build a fire, Aelara assembled their modest tents. Despite their exhaustion, the excitement of their journey and the anticipation of what awaited them in the Elder Mountains fueled their energy.

"Hard to believe we're sleeping under the stars tonight." Wrapping her cloak around herself, Aelara gazed upwards at the emerging celestial bodies. "It's been a long time since we camped out like this."

Josu nodded, thinking back to those countless nights they spent together when they were younger, huddled under the moonlit sky at the farm and sharing stories and dreams. While he longed for the simpler times of their youth, Josu realized that this continuing journey was crucial in shaping their destiny. At fifteen years old, they were old enough to help provide for their families.

With camp set up and a small fire crackling, Josu and Aelara sat down to share a simple meal of dried meat and bread. In the light of the fire, they did their best to enjoy the peaceful night when they both knew their journey would only become more treacherous.

Watching the moon and stars, a sense of contentment eased Josu's chest as he and Aelara told each other stories, dreaming out loud of the places they wanted to go and things they wanted to see. There was so much world outside of Eldoria they hoped to visit one day. Even if they never got the chance, it was still fun to talk about.

"We should reach the Elder Mountains tomorrow." Twisting a stick into the dirt, Josu gazed at the fire, watching the flames flicker against the dark forest. "I can't help but think of what we will find there."

"No matter what it is," Aelara replied, her eyes sparkling in the firelight, "we'll face it together, just like we always have."

With the night growing colder, Josu added more wood to the fire, holding out his hand to help Aelara stand. "We should get to sleep. Tomorrow will be a long day."

Facing a grueling day come morning, they bunkered down in their tents for a much-needed night's rest. He laid awake for a while, listening to the soft sounds of Aelara breathing in the tent beside him and watching the fire through the thin wall of his shelter. Despite the sting of homesickness, he did his best to remain hopeful for what they would find.

He drifted off to sleep as the promise of the unknown beckoned, urging him toward the Elder Mountains even in his dreams, envisioning all the treasures hidden within them.

Chapter 6

Dangers of the Forest

The next morning, Josu awoke to birds singing and the faint rustling of leaves, the air around him still chilly. He blinked, sliding the tent's flap open. Sunlight filtered through the canopy, casting dappled shadows on the forest floor around their tents. Aelara was already awake, her hair tied back in a loose ponytail as she prepared their meager breakfast. Josu stretched and yawned, taking in the scene, feeling a renewed sense of hope as he watched her, their shared goal still at the forefront of his mind. Taking a deep breath, he stepped out of his tent.

"Morning, sleepyhead," she teased, handing him a piece of dried fruit. "We've got a big day ahead."

Rubbing his eyes, Josu nodded and then popped the fruit into his mouth. "You're right. We need to be prepared for anything." He looked around at the forest, its beauty concealing the dangers within. Before they'd set off, his father and brother had sat them down and warned them of the things that lived in the forest—explained how best to stay safe. Their first day in the forest had been uneventful, but he wasn't naive enough to believe the rest of the trip would be as well.

As they packed up and resumed their journey, the terrain grew more treacherous, the Elder Mountains growing ever closer.

The trees loomed taller and twisted, their gnarled roots snaking across the ground, ready to trip any unwary traveler. The air was heavy with humidity, an eerie silence hanging over the forest, as if it were holding its breath in anticipation.

"Josu," Aelara whispered, her eyes scanning the underbrush. "Do you feel like we're being watched?"

He shivered, holding the hilt of his sword tighter. "Yeah, I do. We have to keep moving. Stay close."

Although the hair on the back of his neck prickled, they continued onward, senses heightened by the unnerving atmosphere.

Suddenly, as though coming from everywhere at once, a guttural growl echoed through the woods, and a monstrous creature burst forth from the shadows. The creature was unlike anything Josu had seen before—a hulking mass of muscle and fur, with razor-sharp claws and teeth glinting menacingly in the dappled light.

"Josu, look out!" Aelara yelled, drawing her bow and notching an arrow with practiced ease, aiming it at the creature.

Thinking quickly, Josu lifted his sword, his heart pounding. He glanced at Aelara, determination mirrored in her eyes. "We can do this," he said, steeling himself for the battle, hoping the skills his brother taught him would see him through.

"Stay back, Aelara!" Watching as the creature circled them, drool dripping from its maw, Josu took a defense stance. A second later, it lunged, swiping at him with its massive claws, but Josu dodged just in time, feeling the wind from the near-miss graze his cheek.

"Josu!" Aelara yelled, ignoring his warning and releasing her arrow. It soared through the air, hitting the animal in the shoulder. The creature howled in rage, turning its attention to her, snarling as it prepared to charge.

"Over here, you ugly brute!" Josu taunted, trying to direct the creature's attention away from his friend. He swung his sword, slashing the monster's leg and causing it to stumble. It roared in pain, turning back toward him with fury in its black eyes.

"Keep it distracted, Josu!" Moving quickly, Aelara pulled out another arrow and lined up the shot. "I'll finish it off!"

Doing as he was told, Josu fought to keep the creature at bay, dodging its vicious attacks while Aelara took aim. Sweat poured down his face, muscles screaming as he evaded the beast's relentless onslaught. But he couldn't give up—not when Aelara depended on him.

"Josu, now!" Aelara loosened her arrow with deadly precision, striking the creature in the eye. It let out a final, anguished roar, collapsing to the ground.

"Is... is it dead?" Josu panted, legs trembling.

Approaching cautiously, Aelara nudged the creature with her boot. "Yeah." Relief flooded her features as well. "We did it."

"Thanks to your amazing aim." Josu grinned as he wiped down his sword, his heart rate struggling to slow.

"Couldn't have done it without you watching my back," Aelara replied, smiling as she slung her bow over her shoulder.

For a moment, they stood there, catching their breath and surveying the aftermath of their battle. After such a close call, Josu dropped his sword and pulled Aelara into a hug, relieved she hadn't gotten hurt. They had faced one of the many dangers of the Elder Mountains, and together, they had triumphed. He just hoped they wouldn't face any other attacks on their journey. Returning home in one piece was their top priority.

Chapter 7
Ancient Embrace

With hearts still pounding from the encounter with the monstrous creature, Josu and Aelara pressed on, resolute in their quest to reach the Elder Mountains. The forest gradually yielded to a rocky landscape, where jagged peaks loomed overhead like ancient guardians. As they ascended, the terrain became increasingly treacherous—narrow paths twisted alongside sheer cliffs, and loose rocks threatened to send them tumbling into the abyss below.

"Whoa," Aelara whispered, her eyes filled with wonder as they paused to catch their breath. "The view up here is incredible."

Josu scanned the sprawling landscape below, pride swelling in his chest at their progress. "Yeah, it's something else."

Feeling the exhaustion creeping into their limbs, Josu and Aelara decided to make camp for the night, although they knew it would extend the trip. They found a flat area amidst the craggy rocks, a spot that offered some protection from the mountain winds. Working together, they set up their two tents, securing them against the unpredictable mountain weather.

Once the tents were up, Aelara prepared their dinner and Josu gathered dry branches, creating a warm and welcoming bonfire in the cold mountain air. They sat around the fire, sharing scary stories and reliving the adrenaline-fueled moments of their recent encounter with the creature. The crackling flames cast dancing shadows on the rocky surroundings, creating images that only made their surroundings seem more dangerous.

As the night deepened, fatigue from their challenging journey and the adrenaline of the fight caught up with them. They retreated to their respective tents. Josu was grateful for the shelter and warmth provided by their makeshift camp. The Elder Mountains stood silent and majestic, guarding over the sleeping teens who rested beneath the starlit sky. The next day held the promise of exploring mysterious caves, but for now, Josu and Aelara drifted into a well-deserved and peaceful slumber in the heart of the mountains.

The moment they woke up, Josu and Aelara packed up their camp, stomping on the embers left by the fire to ensure they were extinguished. There was no time to savor the view; their mission awaited and their parents were waiting for their return.

Delving deeper into the mountains, they entered a narrow ravine. Cave openings dotted their path, some appearing impassable. Josu shivered as the landscape sent a chill down his spine, images of creatures lurking in the shadows making his skin crawl—memories of the attack in the forest replaying in his mind. The air held a colder bite than the familiar warmth of his family's farm, carrying with it the scent of damp earth and moss on the breeze. The echo of their footsteps bounced off the stone walls, creating a symphony of sounds that reverberated through the hidden corridors.

Dim light seeped through occasional openings in the rock, casting ethereal shadows that gracefully danced along the uneven surfaces. The stone varied beneath their fingertips, ranging from smooth, worn surfaces to rough, jagged edges. Aelara paused to retrieve the fire starter from her bag, lighting their lantern to guide their way through the darkening passages.

As they cautiously navigated the labyrinthine passages, the distant drip of water echoed—a subtle reminder of unseen underground streams carving their path through the mountain's depths. Josu heightened his senses, attuned to every subtle sound and shift in the environment. The taste of the mountain air felt pure and invigorating, a blend of earthiness and a hint of minerals absent on the farm.

With weapons poised and an air of anticipation, they pressed forward, eager to uncover the mysteries concealed within the mountain's ancient embrace.

"Listen," Aelara whispered, her steps coming to a stop. "Do you hear that?"

Josu strained his ears, discerning a faint, echoing sound—a distant trickle of water or the rustle of some unseen creature.

"Let's follow it." His curiosity sparked. "Maybe it'll lead us to something important."

As they advanced, the sound intensified, guiding them to an enormous chamber bathed in sunlight filtering through cracks in the ceiling. Tapestries of moss and lichen adorned the walls, and the air resonated with the delicate music of dripping water.

"Wow," Josu murmured, eyes wide with awe as he scanned the chamber for signs of danger or hidden treasure. "This place is amazing."

Aelara nodded. "It feels like we're standing in the heart of the mountain."

"Maybe we are." Grinning, Josu ran his fingers along the stone wall. "And if we're lucky, maybe we'll find what we're looking for in here."

"Let's hope so," Aelara said, her eyes widening.

Exploring the chamber, thoughts buzzed in Josu's mind about what might lie hidden within its depths—ancient relics of the long-lost secrets of the Elder Mountains or precious jewels.

"Stay sharp, Aelara." Hand resting on his sword's hilt, Josu strained his eyes to see in the dim light as they ventured deeper into the shadows. "We've seen how dangerous these mountains can be."

"Of course." Lifting her bow, Aelara's fingers tightened on an arrow as she notched it. "But remember, Josu—where there's danger, there's often reward."

With that thought guiding them, they pressed onward, the thrill of adventure coursing through their veins as they ventured deeper into the unknown.

His steps slowing, Josu scanned the cavern walls for any glint of something precious. Aelara stood close by, delicate hands moving along the rough surface. The air was chilly and damp, making the stone walls drip with condensation. Their breaths came out in small clouds as they explored the space.

"Remember what my father said," Josu whispered, voice barely audible above the sound of dripping water echoing through the cave. "The gemstones we seek should have a slight glow to them."

"Right," Aelara murmured, eyes never leaving the rock face. Pulling a small chisel and hammer from her pack, she began to carefully chip away at a promising spot. "I think I see something here."

Josu moved closer, his own tools in his hands instead of his sword. He watched as Aelara removed tiny pieces of rock, revealing a thin vein of glittering blue embedded within the stone. His heart raced with excitement, and he grinned at her. "Looks like we're on the right track."

"Feels like it." Fingers brushing over the exposed vein, Aelara smiled. She shared a look of elation with Josu before they both set to work, each taking one side of the vein and meticulously chipping away at the surrounding rock.

As they worked in tandem, Josu marveled at how well they complemented each other—not just in their quest for the gemstones, but in every aspect of their lives. For as long as they had known each other, they had been inseparable, each one's strengths making up for the other's weaknesses. Best of friends.

"Josu," Aelara said, breaking him from his reverie. "I need your help with this part. It's harder than I thought."

"Of course." Pulling his tool out of the stone, he stepped over to her side. He examined the stubborn piece of rock clinging to the gemstone and then looked at Aelara. "Together?"

"Always," she said, and they brought their chisels down in perfect unison, cracking the stone away and revealing a larger, more vibrant section of the glittering blue gemstone.

Their eyes met, sharing a silent moment of triumph before they resumed their work, determination filling their every movement. As they continued to uncover more of the precious gemstones, Josu realized it wasn't just about the treasure itself—it was about the journey, the trust, and the bond they shared that made this adventure truly worthwhile. And as long as they had that, there was nothing they couldn't achieve.

Chapter 8

Run!

Josu chipped away at the rock wall, hands trembling, breaths short and shallow. Aelara's chisel echoed through the cave, a reassuring reminder of their shared effort. Their hard work was paying off, and the gemstones they found glistened like stars in the dim light. Their families could sell them to buy the things they needed, like food for the animals, and for themselves.

"Josu, do you hear that?" Aelara whispered, her voice quivering ever so slightly.

He paused, straining his ears. At first, all he heard was the steady drip of water, but then he caught it—a low whine, reverberating through the air.

"Stay close." Fear prickling at the back of his neck, Josu gripped his chisel tighter. "We don't know what's out there."

"Maybe it's just the wind," Aelara suggested, though unconvincing. She reached for her bow, notching an arrow.

"Or maybe it's something worse." Eyes darting around the cavern, Josu hoped it was just the wind, but knew it wasn't. "We can't let our guard down."

"Agreed." Moving at his side, Aelara's voice was steady despite the uncertainty.

As they crept further, the whine got louder, more desperate. Josu could almost feel the vibrations, each one sending a shiver down his spine.

"I think… I think whatever it is, is just around this corner." With his breath caught in his throat, Josu took a step ahead of his friend.

"Alright." Aelara nodded, grip tightening on her bow. "On three?"

"One... two... three!" Josu lunged around the corner, chisel raised defensively, while Aelara aimed her arrow at the source of the noice.

"Wait!" Josu cried out, lowering his chisel as he realized what—or who—they'd found. "It's just a puppy!"

Following behind him, Aelara lowered her bow, relief flooding her face. "Poor thing must be scared," she said, stepping closer to the trembling animal. "We should bring it with us. Maybe its lost its mamma."

"Good idea." Putting his tool in his pocket, Josu leaned down and scooped up the shivering pup that couldn't have been more than a few months old. Despite the anxiety still pumping his heart too hard, a surge of warmth filled him at the thought of reuniting it with its family. "Let's keep going, then."

"Lead the way, Josu." Aelara flashed him a brave smile.

With the rescued pup in his arms, Josu led the way deeper into the cave system. The narrow tunnels closed in, making each step feel like venturing further into the heart of a living beast. The air grew colder, and every sound echoed hauntingly.

"Josu," Aelara whispered, voice quivering, "are you sure this is the right way?"

"I think so." Even though he said the words, uncertainty crept into his own voice. "These markings on the walls look similar to some I've seen when visiting Orin's shop in town...like something from people who lived long ago. We have to be careful. There might be more dangers lurking in these caves."

Orin Stoneheart was a scholar who lived in the town near the capital. His shop was filled with old books and artifacts that Josu had seen a few times when passing through with his brother. The pup whined, its fear heightening Josu's anxiety.

"Alright, let's keep moving," Aelara said, taking a step forward. "We can't turn back now."

Josu nodded, swallowing hard. "You're right. We'll find what we're looking for and get out of here. Together."

Pressing onward, the tunnel sloped upwards at a steep incline, and the air grew thinner. They struggled for breath, the pup's whimpers adding to the oppressive atmosphere.

"Josu," Aelara gasped, "I think we're getting close. The gemstones should be just up ahead."

"Good." Legs burning from the uphill trek, Josu did his best to hide his own wheezing. "Just a little further, then."

As the ground leveled out, the arrived in a small chamber, the walls shimmering with veins of colorful gems. Josu gently placed the pup on the ground, allowing it to explore as he and Aelara marveled at the sight.

"Josu, we did it!" Aelara exclaimed. "We found more of the gemstones! Now we can—."

In the midst of her statement, a sudden rumble shook the cave walls. The ground trembled, sending Josu's heart into his stomach as he realized what was happening.

"Run!" he shouted, grabbing Aelara's hand and the pup. They sprinted back down the incline, the walls collapsing behind them, a cacophony of crashing rocks and the ominous roar of the imploding cavern echoing through the narrow passageways.

"Josu!" Aelara screamed, her voice drowned by the deafening chaos. "Will we make it out?"

He didn't answer, fear choking his voice. The darkness seemed to close in around them as they raced against time, the flickering light of the lantern revealing glimpses of the perilous terrain.

The air grew thick with dust, making it hard to breathe as they dodged falling debris and leaped over crevices that seemed to appear out of nowhere. The echoes of their frantic footsteps mixed with the ominous symphony of collapsing rocks and the relentless pursuit of impending danger.

Each passing moment intensified the uncertainty, the walls threatening to crumble upon them. Josu's heart pounded in sync with the rapid beats of their desperate escape. Whether they would emerge from this subterranean ordeal unscathed or succumb to the unforgiving embrace of the collapsing caverns remained unknown. The very essence of danger enveloped them, and the outcome of their harrowing race against the collapsing caves hung in the balance like a precarious thread. The *fate* of Josu, Aelara, and the small pup hung in the balance—and as they ran, Josu worried they wouldn't make it out alive.

Chapter 9

Ancient Arms

Running through the narrow cavern corridors with Aelara by his side, Josu clutched the trembling puppy close to his chest, determined to protect it at all costs. As the shaking intensified, the once-solid ground seemed to betray them, shifting erratically beneath their feet.

"Watch out for the stalagmites!" Aelara warned, narrowly avoiding one herself as she leapt over a fallen rock. "We don't want to get impaled!"

"Thanks for the reminder." Ducking low under a low-hanging stalactite, Josu held the puppy tighter. His mind raced with thoughts of his family, who were unaware of the danger they were in. He couldn't fail them or Aelara.

He couldn't fail the puppy. They had to make it out alive.

"Almost there," Aelara yelled as the path appeared to open up yards before them, breath coming in ragged pants. "Just a little further!"

But as they ran, Josu couldn't shake the growing sense of dread that weighed heavily upon him. What if they didn't make it out in time? What if the cave collapsed, trapping them inside forever? The thought alone was enough to make his limbs numb.

"No," he told himself, pushing those terrifying images away. "We'll make it. We *have* to."

As they stumbled over the last of the jagged rocks and dodged treacherous stalagmites in their path, Josu focused all his energy into reaching safety. The echoing footsteps of their frantic escape seemed to chase them, urging them to move faster. And with each passing second, the shaking grew stronger, threatening to swallow them whole.

"Josu!" Aelara cried out as she tripped over a loose stone, quickly regaining her footing and continuing to run. "We're almost there!"

He spared a glance back, relieved to see that she was still right behind him. With renewed determination, he sprinted faster than he ever had before, his heart pounding like a wild drum.

It felt like an eternity, but finally, the opening got closer, a beacon of hope in the midst of chaos. As they hurtled toward it, the ground beneath them continued to tremble, its angry roars echoing through the cavernous space.

"Come on!" Josu yelled, desperation seeping into his voice. He could feel the puppy's accelerated heartbeat against his chest, mirroring his own. They were so close to safety, so painfully close.

With one final surge of strength, Josu and Aelara burst out of the narrow space just as the shaking made its grand finale, leaving broken bits of stone along the path, their breaths ragged and their hearts racing.

"Are you okay?" Josu asked, turning to Aelara, who nodded. The relief in her eyes mirrored his own, and for a moment, they simply stood there, catching their breath and processing what had just happened.

"Never again." Panting, a weak smile forming on Aelara's lips. "Let's never do that again."

"Agreed," Josu whispered, holding the puppy a little closer.

Josu and Aelara, still trying to catch their breath from their harrowing escape, cautiously ventured farther into the depths of the cave. The shaking had subsided, and they found themselves in a large, beautiful cavern bathed in a soft, ethereal glow coming from a crack in the ceiling.

"Wow," Josu whispered, his eyes wide with wonder. "Have you ever seen anything like this before?"

"Never." Aelara's voice was tinged with awe as her eyes scanned the sparkling chamber. "It's like there's magic here."

The cavern's towering stalactites and stalagmites seemed to reach for one another, like ancient arms frozen in time. The shadows they cast danced gracefully on the walls, creating an air of mystery that made Josu's heart race with excitement.

"Look at the light." Setting the lantern on the floor, Aelara pointed at the source of the glow. Small, luminescent insects fluttered about, illuminating the cavern with their delicate wings.

"Amazing." Josu watched them, entranced by their beauty.

"Josu, do you think we should tell your parents about this place?" she asked, interrupting his thoughts.

Torn between wanting to share this incredible discovery and fearing the potential consequences, he hesitated for a moment. "I don't know. We already risked our lives just getting here. I don't know if I want them to come back here, especially not after the quake."

Chapter 10
Thrill of Discovery

"Josu, over here!" Aelara's voice resonated through the cavern as she gestured toward the adjacent wall. Josu blinked, adjusting his eyes to the cave's ambient glow, focusing on the intriguing sight that had captivated her.

Intricate markings adorned the walls, weaving a tapestry of ancient symbols that hinted at a long-forgotten narrative. The lines twisted and curved, creating a mesmerizing dance of shapes. "This is unlike anything I've seen before," he murmured, tracing the cool, smooth etchings with his fingers, conveying an age beyond comprehension.

"Agreed." The wonder was reflected in her wide eyes as she did the same. "Could these be connected to the cave somehow? A hidden secret or power, perhaps?"

"Possibly." Curiosity ignited, Josu pondered the thought. He envisioned the untold stories concealed within these symbols, revealing the cavern's enigmatic past.

As they delved deeper into exploring the cryptic markings, their footsteps led them farther into the cavern's depths. Soft light bathed stalactites and stalagmites, casting a myriad of colors, creating an otherworldly ambiance.

"Josu, look down!" Aelara's sudden exclamation diverted his attention to the cavern floor, a gasp leaving his mouth at the dazzling display.

Gems of various shapes and sizes were scattered across the floor, reflecting the ethereal illumination. Blues, greens, reds, and oranges sparkled, each gem pulsating with a unique inner light. With every step, the gems shifted, creating a symphony of colors around them.

"Wow." Josu squatted to examine a particularly large gem emitting an inner fire. "I didn't think it could get any more amazing in here."

"I didn't either." Excitement shined in Aelara's eyes as she picked up a brilliant blue stone. "This place is like something out of a fairy tale."

Josu nodded, overwhelmed by the spectacle. The gems, ancient markings, and the breathtaking cavern coalesced into an unforgettable experience.

Amidst the thrill of discovery, Josu's thoughts turned inward. Questions about the cave's mysterious origins and their implications for the future raced through his mind. What secrets were concealed within these walls, and what consequences awaited if they dared to unlock them?

As he thought, Josu scanned the cavern floor, gems sparkling like stars beneath his feet. When he picked up another iridescent stone, his attention shifted to an unexpected sight: a larger object nestled among the gems, partially obscured by shimmering colors.

"Hey, Aelara," he called out. "Come take a look at this."

Aelara hurried over, her eyebrows furrowed. "What did you find?"

"Look." With a gentle touch, he carefully moved aside some of the gems, revealing a large egg-like object. The brilliant surface, covered in shimmering scales, changed color as they moved.

"Is that..." Aelara's voice trailed off, eyes wide with astonishment.

"Could it really be?" Despite his hesitation, Josu reached out to touch the warm, pulsating object.

"Josu, it's a dragon egg!" Aelara exclaimed, unable to contain her excitement.

"But... dragons are supposed to be extinct in Eldoria." Mind racing from the discovery, his voice trailed off as he spoke the next few words. "Maybe even in the world."

"Maybe we should leave it here." Aelara stepped back, lifting the puppy from the ground and petting its duty coat. "Taking it with us could bring trouble."

Josu hesitated, eyeing the beautiful egg. After a moment, he swallowed back his doubts. "No. We can't just leave it here. We need to understand why it's here and what it means. We need to know what's really inside of it. Maybe it's not a dragon egg at all. Whatever it is, it's too beautiful to leave behind."

"Are you sure that's a good idea, Josu?" Aelara's worry was evident on her face as she took a step back.

Clutching the dragon egg, Josu envisioned the potential consequences, realizing the gravity of the discovery as he shared a look with his friend.

"Josu," Aelara whispered, eyes darting around the cavern. "What if keeping this egg endangers not just us, but our families? We can't risk everyone we care about. We don't know what its inside of it, or if it's dangerous."

He knew she was right, yet the possibility of uncovering the egg's secrets held him. Closing his eyes, he pictured his mother's face, sadness creeping into his chest at how much he missed her. Still, the thought of leaving his treasure behind sent pain into his stomach.

"Josu?" Aelara's voice softened. "Are we doing the right thing?"

"Maybe not," he replied, meeting her gaze. "But we have a responsibility to uncover the truth. What if this egg holds something that can help our families, or our kingdom? If we leave it, we may never get another chance."

Aelara bit her lip, seeming to consider his words before nodding. "Alright, but we need a plan. How do we keep this secret safe and investigate without drawing attention?"

Sliding the object into his satchel, Josu blew out a breath. "I don't know, but we have a long hike home to figure it out."

Chapter 11

Precious Cargo

With heavy satchels, Josu and Aelara emerged from the caves, legs weakened by exhaustion. The moment they were clear of the structure, he leaned against the rocky entrance for support, his face and clothes smeared with sweat and dirt. Beside him, Aelara appeared with a sigh of relief, wiping her brow.

"Finally," she gasped, "I thought we'd never make it out of there."

"Me too." Placing the puppy on the ground, he blew out a breath, allowing the remnants of fear to dissipate. As they caught their breath, the lush forest surrounding them came alive. Golden sunlight filtered through the verdant leaves above, illuminating the forest floor in patches. The vibrant green foliage swayed gently in the breeze, while birds chirped merrily in the distance, creating a soothing symphony. Even the puppy yipped, so Aelara set it on the ground beside her. To Josu's surprise, it didn't run away.

"Josu," Aelara said, breaking the silence, "I can't believe we actually found one."

"Neither can I." As Josu leaned down to pet the puppy, his thoughts raced. He couldn't shake off the responsibility that weighed heavily on his shoulders. What if they were making a mistake?

"Hey." Aelara nudged him gently, seeming to sense his unease. "We'll figure this out together, alright?"

Appreciating her unwavering support, Josu managed a small smile. "Are you ready to start heading home?"

"Absolutely," she replied, her sharp green eyes scanning the forest around them. Despite her confident words, Josu could see the smallest hint of worry in her expression.

Amidst the tranquil beauty of the forest, Josu reflected in their journey thus far. They had been through so much, yet they still had to hike all the way back home. Although they'd already faced dangers and challenges, he knew more could find them on their journey.

With the sun still in the sky, the duo decided to venture a back into the forest, using the map they'd gotten from Josu's father to navigate their way. It wasn't long before the sound of running water reached their ears. Following the gentle melody, they discovered a crystal-clear stream winding through the trees. The water beckoned to them, offering a refreshing respite after the harrowing ordeal in the caves.

Setting up camp near the stream, they took turns washing off the grime and sweat of their adventure. They took turns washing up as the puppy splashed about, adding an unexpected element of playfulness to the scene.

As the sun dipped below the horizon, they gathered dry branches for a bonfire and then Aelara started the fire while Josu set up their tents. They cooked a simple meal of salted meat over the flames, the scent mingling with the crisp forest air and making the puppy cry for a bite.

Sitting around the fire, they ate, sharing their food with Bandit, a name Aelara picked out after much discussion about how the puppy hiding in the shadows reminded her of a robber. The night sky above twinkled with stars, providing a celestial backdrop to their impromptu campsite, setting Josu at ease even though he realized there were dangers hiding in the darkness.

Eventually, fatigue caught up with them, and they retired to their tents for the night. The forest embraced them in a peaceful stillness as they settled into a well-deserved sleep, the events of the day fading into dreams.

The next morning, recharged and determined, Josu and Aelara broke camp and began the long hike back to their village. The forest, now bathed in the soft light of dawn, seemed to whisper tales of their adventures as they trekked homeward, their newfound discovery tucked safely in their hearts, and the mysterious egg hiding in Josu's bag.

We've got a lot of work ahead of us," Aelara said, giving Josu a reassuring pat on the back.

"Right." Josu's heart pounded with anticipation as they ventured deeper into the forest, leaving the clearing by the stream far behind them. As they continued their trek through the forest, the sun-kissed leaves cast dappled patterns on the soft earth beneath their feet. The peacefulness of the surroundings embraced Josu like a comforting blanket, providing a much-needed reprieve from the chaos they had left behind.

"Josu." Brushing a stray lock of hair back from her face, Aelara seemed to hesitate. "I can't believe we actually made it out of there alive. For a little while, I was really scared."

"Me too," he admitted, the familiar ache of homesickness settling in his chest. He couldn't help but glance down at their precious cargo nestled securely in his bag, his eyes lingering on the faint tracing of veins that hinted at the life within.

"Hey." Aelara nudged him with her sholder, her lips lifting into a small smile. "We'll be okay from now on. We just have to be extra careful."

Tightening his hold on his sword, Josu nodded. "I know. It's just a little unbelievable."

"Remember when we used to play hide and seek in these woods?" Aelara said, absent-mindedly kicking a pebble along the worn path. "We never would have guessed we'd end up carrying something so... extraordinary."

His mind racing with memories of their innocent adventures, Josu shook his head. "Never."

As they drew closer to his family's farm, the familiar sights and smells of home began to emerge. The scent of freshly turned soil mingled with the sweet fragrance of blooming wildflowers, while the distant hum of bees promised a bountiful harvest.

"Look." Aelara pointed to the hazy outline of the farmhouse up ahead. "We're almost there."

"Finally." Relief washed over Josu as they stepped onto the well-trodden path leading to his family's land. The sight of the familiar white building, its wooden exterior weathered by years of sun and wind, brought a sense of security that seemed to melt away the tension in his shoulders.

"Josu!" his mother called from the porch, wiping her hands on her apron. "I was starting to worry about you two. You were supposed to be back yesterday."

"Sorry, Mom." Josu waved, trying to sound more at ease than he felt. "We just got a little... sidetracked."

"Come inside," she beckoned, narrowing her eyes at their dirt-streaked faces and the wiggling puppy in Aelara's hands. "You can wash up while I finish making dinner."

"I'll have to head home soon," Aelara said, sharing a conspiratorial look with Josu. "My dad is probably worried."

Chapter 12
The Hiding Spot

"Wait," Josu whispered, gripping Aelara's arm as they walked into the farmhouse kitchen. His mother, oblivious to their covert mission, continued to stir the pot on the stove. "We need to hide it before dinner."

Alera nodded, her eyes flicking to the old barn visible through the window, the sunset illuminating it like a beacon. "Good idea. Let's go."

"Mom, we're just going put our things away and take Bandit to potty," Josu said as he opened the back door, hoping his mother didn't hear the anxiety in his tone.

Not looking up from the pot in front of her, his mother nodded. "Alright, but don't take too long!"

Slipping out the back door of the farmhouse, Josu and Aelara traversed the field toward the old barn, its weathered wooden walls making it blend with the forest behind it. The creaking doors seemed to beckon them inside, promising to keep their secret safe within.

"Come on," Aelara urged, nudging Josu forward and closing the door behind them.

Entering the dimly lit interior, the musty scent of hay and old wood filled Josu's nostrils. He crossed the room and opened the window, needing to air out the room and bring in light. Aelara followed, setting the puppy on the ground.

"Okay, let's find a good spot." Josu's heart raced as he pulled the dragon egg out of his bag and cradled it in his hands

"Over there." Scanning the shadowed interior, Aelara pointed to a secluded corner behind hay bales. "Hidden from view, and there's enough hay for a soft bed."

"Perfect." Relief loosened Josu's muscles as they made their way to the hiding spot, even as excitement buzzed through his veins. Bandit followed close behind them, his nose buried in the dirt as he sniffed every square inch of space. Once in the corner, they arranged the hay, creating a secure nest for the dragon egg.

"Is this good?" Josu asked, hesitating before lowering the precious cargo into its new home.

Picking up the yapping puppy, Aelara nodded. "Yeah, it looks great. No one will find it here."

"Good." With a dip of his chin, Josu covered the egg with hay and stepped back, hoping their handiwork would hide their treasure until they devised a better plan. He wondered if he was truly ready for such a responsibility, but the anticipation of what lay within the egg drove him forward, determined to see it through.

However, once the task of covering the egg was complete, he hesitated for a moment, staring at the space where the object lay hidden.

"Josu, are you okay?" Aelara's voice pulled him back to the present as they stood in the silence, staring at the hay.

"Y-yeah," he stammered, unable to tear his gaze away from the egg. His thoughts raced with a mixture of wonder and worry—had he made a mistake bringing such a powerful creature into their lives? Yet the possibility of forming an unbreakable bond with the dragon was a temptation he couldn't resist, if the egg hatched at all. No matter how badly he wanted to see a dragon for himself, he knew there was still the possibility that the egg was too old to still have viable life inside. "I just... I hope we're doing the right thing. And you should take Bandit home with you. He likes you better anyway."

Aelara smiled, petting the puppy's coat as it leaned into her hand. She placed a reassuring hand on his shoulder, the light streaming in from the window brightening her smile, her eyes sparkling in the setting sun. "He likes us both, but I would love to take him home with me. He can learn to be a guard dog. And don't worry about the egg right now, Josu. It may not even hatch, but if it does, you can always talk to Orin Stoneheart about it. You've seen his shop in town. He knows everything there is to know about dragons."

"Thanks, Aelara," he whispered, grateful for her unwavering support.

A sudden bark from the puppy reminded them of the passage of time. Aelara picked it up gently, holding it in her arms. "I should get going," she said, clearing her throat when her voice broke. "My dad will be wondering where I am."

"Right." Josu nodded, swallowing the lump in his throat. "Be careful heading home, Aelara." Trying to mask his own feelings of loss and loneliness at her departure, he offered her a small smile. After their journey together, he'd grown used to her being by his side. She didn't live far, but he knew he would still miss her.

"I will." When she turned to leave, her eyes were glassy as though she was sad to go too.

"We'll venture out again soon, and when we do, we'll have the adventure of a lifetime."

"Josu!" his mother's voice echoed outside the barn door, cutting through the field. "Dinner's almost ready!"

"Coming, Mom!" Lifting his gaze to the open window, he exchanged a quick, nervous glance with Aelara.

"Let's go," she whispered, nudging him with her shoulder. "You can check on it after dinner."

Although he was hesitant to let their treasure out of his sight, when his mother hollered again, Josu nodded.

Chapter 13

The Secret

Josu's heart ached as he watched Aelara's retreating figure, her flaming red hair dancing behind her like flickering embers. The puppy wriggled in her arms, its tiny face peeking out and staring at him with its big eyes. As they vanished into the distance, a pang of uncertainty settled within him. He and Aelara had taken on the dragon egg together, and without her there, it was just him.

Standing there, the sounds of the forest drifted through the air—birds chirping and leaves rustling in the wind—but they did little to soothe his troubled thoughts.

Before heading inside, he glanced back at the old barn, its wooden surface crumbling from the years. The treasure inside was worth so much more than the building that housed it. In the morning, he knew he needed to find a better hiding spot for it.

Opening the back door of the farmhouse, his heart pounded in tandem with the rhythmic stirring sound his mother made as she cooked over the stove. The aroma of simmering vegetables and herbs wafted through the air, filling Josu's nostrils and tugging at his stomach, reminding him that he hadn't eaten since that morning. His mother turned to smile at him, her eyes crinkling at the corners.

"Are you ready for dinner, kiddo?" she asked, placing a wooden spoon on the counter.

"Starving." Although anxiety twisted his stomach, he forced a grin onto his face in an attempt to hide the weight of the secret he carried. Stepping into the cozy kitchen, he pulled out a chair and settled down at the table. As he looked around the room, the familiar sense of warmth and belonging washed over him like a comforting blanket. He loved his adventures, but missed home when he was away.

"Your father and brother will be back shortly," his mother said, her voice soothing the tension in his chest. "They're just finishing up with the last of the chores in the back fields."

"Thanks, Mom." His gaze lingered on the empty seat across from him. It was where Aelara would usually sit when she had dinner with them, her eyes twinkling with mischief as they exchanged stories about their day. He missed her already, but he knew he had to focus on the task at hand—protecting the dragon egg.

"Josu, are you alright?" Concern etched lines on his mother's forehead as she searched his face. "You seem a bit distracted."

"Uh, yeah. I'm fine, just tired." With a nod, he rubbed the back of his neck, wincing at the grime that had gathered there. After dinner, he knew he needed a bath. "We made it all the way to the mountains, looking for treasures."

"And did you find any treasures?" his mother asked, her lips tipping up in a smile that brought one to his own. "And were the two of you careful? Because that's what's really important, Josu. That you and Aelara were careful."

"We're always careful, Mom. You know boys my age already serve in the king's guard." Even as he said the words, his stomach lurched with guilt as he realized that his family had no idea what lay hidden in the barn. He may have been old enough to serve for the king, but a dragon was a bigger responsibility than any one person could handle. He knew that, but he still wanted to keep it.

Sliding his hand into his bag on the floor, he pulled out a few of the gemstones that lay within. "I did find treasures though, Mom. These can help the family, right?"

His mother's eyes grew wide as she slid down into the char next to him, her fingers reaching out to touch the blue stone. "Josu, this is—"

Footsteps echoed outside. A moment later, his father and brother filed into the kitchen, his father's eyes widening when he noticed the gemstones on the table. Pride filled Josu's chest at the look on his family's face, knowing he'd found something to help support them.

"Josu, did you find these?" Reaching forward, his father scooped them up, bringing the three stones closer to his eyes. "This can pay for the animal's feed for a year, my boy. How—."

Tears brimmed his mother's eyes as they watched the stones sparkle in the lantern light of the kitchen, moisture dripping down her cheek.

Despite the uncertainties that lingered in his mind, he knew at that moment—sitting down to eat dinner with his family—that his family would always support and love him, no matter what his future held.

"You've really helped our family with these, Josu," Rennan said, reaching over to ruffle Josu's hair. "I always knew you were brave and resourceful. You've proved it tonight."

Warmth blooming in his chest, a smile spread across Josu's face, although he knew that soon, nothing would ever be the same. Still, until things changed, he would cherish every moment of happiness and love, gathering strength for the challenges that awaited him and his new charge nestled in the barn.

Chapter 14

Early Riser

The next morning, Josu stirred with the dawn's first light, opening his eyes before the roosters crowed. A sense of purpose and responsibility swept over him as he swung his legs over the bed, his bare feet meeting the cool wooden floor. It was another day on the farm, yet the day seemed to hold a significance beyond the routine of tending to crops and animals. Sure, he had to work on the farm, but he'd provided for his family in a way that he'd never been able to before, and that meant everything to him.

Eager to make the most of the early morning hours before the sun reached its peak, he dressed in his worn work clothes, laced up his boots, and then grabbed a homemade egg biscuit from the kitchen counter. Stepping outside, he breathed in the fresh air. The sun, just beginning its ascent, shone over the fields with its golden glow as the world was still half-asleep. Silence prevailed, interrupted only by the occasional chirp of an awakening bird or the rustle of leaves in the gentle breeze.

Josu smiled, appreciating the beauty of the world around him and grateful for the simplicity of his life on the farm. However, amidst the serenity, persistent thoughts about the dragon egg he had discovered lingered in his mind. He glanced toward the old barn, wanting to go check on it, to make sure it was still undisturbed, but the last thing he wanted was for his father to follow him in and discover his secret.

Tackling his chores, he tried to set aside the distracting thoughts. There would be time later to unravel the mysteries of the egg. For the moment, he needed to concentrate on the tasks essential to maintaining the farm and helping his father.

Pushing thoughts of the egg aside, he followed the gravel path to the main barn, his footsteps harmonizing with the awakening nature. The rising sun illuminated the dew-kissed grass, the temperature already warming under its embrace.

"Morning, Josu!' His father's cheerful voice greeted him from where he worked with the animals, pouring slop into troughs for the pigs.

"Early riser today?"

"Couldn't sleep." Rubbing the back of his head sheepishly, Josu squinted against the sun's already vibrant rays. "Thought I'd get a head start on the chores."

"Always good to have a helping hand." His father smiled, leading one of their goats into the feeding yard. "Finish feeding the animals and ensure they have fresh water, will you?"

"Sure thing." Eager to be useful, he nodded. While he worked, he scanned the land around him for his brother, but he didn't see him in the fields. "Did Rennan return to the capital?"

Pouring grain into the troughs, he watched as the chickens pecked away. A sense of pride swelled within him, acknowledging his responsibility toward the animals.

His father's footsteps smacked against the damp ground as he returned to where Josu was working. "Rennan left early this morning to bring the gemstones to a trader closer to the city. He should be back this evening. Did your mother tell you about old Farmer McGinty? Found a nest of snake eggs in his hayloft last week."

"Really?" Josu's eyes widened in surprise, his chest tightening when the worry of the same thing happening at their farm crept into his mind. If his father found the dragon egg, it was possible he would think it was a snake egg too, and would destroy it.

"Yup. Had to call in an expert to remove them safely. You never know what you might find around here."

The thought of his father calling in someone to search the property for snake eggs made his stomach turn.

"Josu? Are you alright, son?"

"Uh, yeah. I'm fine." Forcing the thoughts away, Josu smiled. "Just... well... hope he got rid of the snakes, I guess."

"Ah, don't let it bother you too much," his father said, patting Josu on the back. "We'll keep an eye out for anything unusual."

"Right." Josu nodded, swallowing hard as he turned his attention to filling water buckets for the animals.

As he worked, the weight of his secret bore down on him. Yet, in the quiet moments between splashing water and the contented sounds of the animals, he found solace in the knowledge that he was not alone in facing the challenges ahead. With that thought, his resolve only strengthened.

"Alright, Dad," he said, his voice firm and steady. "What's next on the list?"

Chapter 15

The Bond

The moon cast a silvery glow over the farm, its light filtering through the leaves of the trees and dancing on the ground like ghostly shadows. Josu, dressed in worn-out boots and a nightshirt, crept out of the farmhouse, careful not to make any noise that would alert his family. His heart pounded, breath coming in short, shallow gasps as he ventured into the night with a lantern to light his way.

"Josu, where are you off to?" a voice whispered, startling him. He turned around, eyes widening as he saw his brother standing behind him, his eyebrows pinched.

"Just for a walk." Hoping his brother didn't want to join him, Josu's chest tightened. "Couldn't sleep."

"Alright then, be careful," Rennan said, giving him a curious look before disappearing back inside the house.

The moment the door shut between them, Josu exhaled, relieved to have avoided suspicion, at least for the moment. Picking up his pace, he reached the barn within minutes, going directly to the place where he'd left the egg, tension releasing in his stomach when he saw it still nestled among the golden straw. Its surface shimmered with an iridescent sheen, captivating Josu with its beauty. He reached out, gently running his fingers along the cool surface.

With a sigh, he sank down onto the hay beside the egg. He couldn't deny the bond he felt with the creature growing inside, *if* it was growing inside, but the risks were undeniable. Raising a dragon could bring peril to his family and their farm, and yet, he couldn't bring himself to turn away from it. The egg called to him. Its presence was a constant hum in the back of his mind, a reminder of the responsibility he now bore.

"Josu," the voice came again, this time louder than before. "What are you doing in there? That old barn could collapse any moment. It's not safe."

"Nothing!" Hastily covering the egg with a layer of hay, he scrambled to his feet, trying to look as innocent as possible as he jogged back toward the doorway.

"Is everything alright?" his brother asked, approaching him from the back of the barn.

"Of course." Josu forced a smile. "Just restless, that's all."

"Maybe you should get some sleep," Rennan said, reaching out to ruffle Josu's hair. "We've got a long day ahead of us tomorrow. Plus, there's lightning in the sky to the east. A storm is coming."

"Okay."

Leaving the egg behind, his heart was heavy with unspoken secrets, but he followed Rennan toward the house in silence. Before he walked back inside, he couldn't help but cast one last glance at the barn, the weight of his decision settling around him like a cloak.

"Goodnight, Josu," his brother said, disappearing into the darkness once more.

Josu closed the door behind them, following his brother toward his bedroom. "Goodnight."

A deafening crack split the night, followed by a frantic pounding on Josu's door. He jolted awake, heart pounding in his chest as his father's urgent voice pierced through the darkness.

"Josu! The old barn is on fire! We need your help!"

Without hesitation, he scrambled out of bed, adrenaline pumping through his veins. As he threw open the door, his mother rushed past him, clutching a bucket in her trembling hands. "The flames are spreading, Josu! Hurry!"

The urgency in their voices propelled him into action. He sprinted toward the old barn, the smell of smoke and the distant flicker of flames growing stronger with each step. Panic clawed at his throat, but he pushed it down, focusing on his duty to his family

"Josu, grab that bucket!" his father shouted over the roar of the fire. Josu obeyed without thought, joining the desperate effort to douse the flames with water from the nearby well.

As they fought against the inferno, a horrifying thought struck Josu like a bolt of lightning—he'd left the lantern in the barn when his brother had called him before they'd gone to bed. When he'd walked away to follow Rennan, the dragon egg was still hidden among the hay bales inside the barn. His breath hitched, and for a moment, he couldn't move or speak. Despair and guilt swirled within him, threatening to consume him like the fire itself. *It was all his fault.*

"No," he whispered, unwilling to accept the possibility that the egg could be lost forever. Ever since he'd found it in the caves, he'd treasured it, waiting for it to hatch and hoping it would. And now, just as he had started to feel a connection with the life inside, everything might be reduced to ashes. It was unthinkable.

"Josu, focus!" his father urged, snapping him out of his thoughts. "We can't let this fire spread to the rest of the farm!"

Shaking off the crushing weight of despair, Josu pushed his self-blame to the back of his mind, focusing on putting out the fire. He couldn't afford to let his family down, even if it meant sacrificing the dragon egg. As he threw bucket after bucket of water onto the flames, he clung to a small sliver of hope that maybe, just maybe, the egg could somehow survive the blaze. But deep down, as the fire roared and danced around him, Josu couldn't escape the feeling that he was losing something precious, something that could never be replaced.

Chapter 16
Miracle in the Ashes

The last flames surrendered to the water's assault, leaving behind a scorched and blackened scene. Josu stood there, catching his breath, surveying the ruin that was once their old barn. The smell of smoke lingered in the air, clinging to his hair and clothes. A hand rested on his shoulder, and he looked up into his father's tired, soot-streaked face.

"Good job, son," his father said, his voice hoarse from shouting and coughing. "We've done what we can for now. Let's get some rest."

With nothing else to do outside, the family made their way back to the house. Josu glanced over his shoulder at the smoldering ruins, bathed in an eerie moonlight that made everything appear as haunted as his thoughts. The ashes seemed to shimmer, as if the fire still lurked beneath, waiting for a chance to rise again. Shivering from the night chill, he hurried after his family.

Inside, they slumped around the kitchen table, their exhaustion palpable. His mother handed out cups of warm milk with slow, deliberate movements. Silence hung heavy with unspoken thoughts and worries. When they finished their drinks and retired to bed, Josu found sleep elusive. The image of the destroyed barn and the dragon egg he'd lost plagued him.

"Maybe there's still a chance," he thought, staring at the ceiling. "I have to know."

Josu waited until his family's steady breathing filled the house. Sliding out of bed, he pulled on his boots and grabbed a lantern. His heart pounded as he approached the remains of the barn, his stomach clenching with anxiety of the unknown.

Stepping over the charred remains, he searched through ash and wood, hands blackened with soot. His breath caught as he uncovered a scorched bale of hay, the hiding place for the dragon egg. The suspense coiled within him like a spring ready to snap.

"Please, be there," he repeated, digging deeper.

As if by miracle, his fingers brushed against something warm and solid—the unmistakable curve of the dragon egg. He pulled it from the wreckage, awe and relief washing over him. Somehow, it was unscathed. The fire had spared it.

Blowing out a breath, he cradled the egg gently. Its survival seemed unbelievable.

"Are you in there?" he whispered. "Can you hear me?"

As if responding, a faint crack appeared on the egg's surface, cutting through the iridescent sheen. Josu's heart leaped into his throat as the crack grew larger, splitting the air with a sound like thunder. Tightening his grip on the egg, he watched as the crack widened, revealing something extraordinary within.

With a burst of energy, the shell shattered, and Josu stared into the eyes of a creature unlike anything he had ever seen—a baby dragon small enough to fit in his hand, its delicate wings coated in eggshell remnants. Its scales shimmered in the lantern light, reflecting hues of copper, like the color of fire in the darkness.

"Wow. You're beautiful."

The dragon blinked, its eyes shimmering like the sea as it took in the world for the first time.

"Hey there, little one," he whispered, reaching out a finger to stroke its velvety-soft head. "I'm Josu. I'm going to take care of you."

As if understanding his words, the baby dragon gave a soft chirp, nuzzling against Josu's finger. A bond formed in that moment—one forged by fire and ash, by hope and fate.

"Welcome to the world," he whispered, his heart swelling with love for the tiny creature. "I'll name you Kenna," he whispered into the dragon's ear, naming her after the fire that had brought her into the world. "But you have to stay quiet, okay? We need to be sneaky."

In the moonlight, Josu surveyed his family's small cottage, his heart racing as he held the baby dragon close to his chest. Getting her to safety without detection felt nearly impossible in their cramped home.

Kenna chirped softly, nuzzling against Josu's shirt as if to express understanding. Taking a deep breath, he tiptoed across the house, ducking behind furniture and pausing to listen for any signs of his family.

The moment his bedroom door closed behind them, the baby dragon wriggled free from his grip, stretching her wings and giving an experimental flutter.

He huffed a laugh, scooping her up, and tucking her into a makeshift nest of blankets in the corner of his room. "Tomorrow, we'll go see Orin Stoneheart. He knows everything about dragon lore. He can help us."

Chapter 17
The Flame Riders

With a cloak pulled over his head and the baby dragon tucked within, Josu knocked on Orin Stoneheart's door the next morning, excitement flowing through him like a bubbling stream.

When the older man opened the door, surprise lifted his thick, gray eyebrows. "Hello, young Josu. What brings you to my doorstep today?"

"Orin, I... I need your help," Josu blurted out, the weight of responsibility for Kenna and the secrets he was keeping from his family pressing down on him. "I found something amazing, and I think you might be the only one who can help me."

"Ah, is that so?" Stepping aside Orin stroked his long white beard. "Well, come in then. Let's see what this mystery is all about."

Once inside, Josu could hardly contain himself. It felt as if every cell in his body was buzzing with adrenaline. He glanced around at the old books lining the walls and the artifacts placed carefully on shelves—evidence of Orin's vast knowledge of Eldorian history and dragon lore.

"Alright," Josu whispered, gently pulling back his cloak to reveal Kenna, a trill leaving her mouth as she stretched her wings. Her shimmering scales seemed to catch Orin's breath, leaving him momentarily speechless.

"By the gods," Orin finally gasped, his eyes wide with amazement. "A dragon! Where on earth did you find her, Josu?"

"In the mountains." Holding Kenna out in front of Orin, Josu's voice shook with both pride and nerves. "I found her egg in the caves, but she hatched after a barn fire last night."

"Extraordinary." Orin leaned in for a closer look at her. "You have no idea how rare this is, young one. Dragons haven't been seen in Eldoria for centuries."

As Orin studied Kenna, Josu's mind raced with questions. What did it mean to care for a dragon? How could he protect her? What did this mean for his family, his friends—his entire world?

"Can you help me, Orin?" Hope flickered in his chest like a candle's flame as he watched Kenna nuzzle Orin's fingers. "I need to know how to raise Kenna properly and keep her safe."

"Indeed." Orin's gaze softened as he placed his hand on Josu's shoulder. "I will do my best to guide you, Josu. This is an incredible responsibility, but I believe that you are up to the challenge."

"Thank you." Relief washed over Josu like a cool breeze on a hot summer day. "Thank you so much."

"First things first," Orin said, straightening up and pulling a dusty book from one of the shelves. "Let us begin your education in the ways of dragons. There is much to learn, and time is of the essence. She will grow up quickly."

For hours, Josu and Orin read through the book, learning about dragon myths and history. They discussed ways to care for a dragon—the importance of proper nutrition, things to look out for in terms of health and well-being, and how to ensure that Kenna was trained to follow his orders and not harm anyone. Orin taught Josu how dragons were once believed to be guardians of Eldoria—powerful creatures who could bring both great joy and great destruction, if not handled with care.

He spoke of legends of brave knights who rode on the backs of dragons into battle against evil forces, the *Flame Riders*, their courage inspiring generations of Eldorians. He shared stories of dragons soaring through the skies—mysterious creatures whose beauty was second only to their might.

As Orin spoke, a sense of wonder swelled inside Josu, rivaling what he felt when he had stepped into the cavern where he'd found her. He had always known dragons were something special, but now he knew just how special they truly were. With Orin's help, he knew he would do whatever it took to protect Kenna and ensure that she could live up to her potential as a great dragon.

As the day wore on, Josu's mind buzzed with newfound knowledge. Together, he and Orin had mapped out a plan for Kenna's care and protection. They had agreed to meet again soon, to continue their lessons and discuss any challenges that might arise.

"Thank you, Orin, for helping me" Josu's heart was full of gratitude for the older man's guidance as he tucked his new friend into his cloak and stepped toward the door.

"You are welcome, my boy," Orin replied, his eyes twinkling with pride. "Remember, this is a great responsibility you have taken on. But with a good heart and hard work, you can do it. You can become a Flame Rider."

To be continued

Also By

Hazel Watson Mystery Series
Kindred Spirits: Prequel
The Sapphire Necklace
Justice for the Slain
Whispers from the Swamp
Crossroads of Death
The Spirit Collector

Crown of the Phoenix Series
Crown of the Phoenix
Crown of the Exiled
Crown of the Prophecy (Coming Soon)
Mate of the Phoenix
Shadowed by Prophecy

Supernatural Savior Series
Song of Death
Goddess of Death

An Other World Series
The Other World
The Other Key
The Other Fate (coming February 2024)

My Alien Mate Series
My Alien Protector

Saving Scarlett (coming January 2024)

Second Chance with Santa (coming December 2024)

About the Author

Raised in a small town in the heart of Louisiana's Cajun Country, C. A. Varian spent most of her childhood fishing, crabbing, and getting sunburnt at the beach. Her love of reading began very young, and she would often compete at school to read enough books to earn prizes. Graduating with the first of her college degrees as a mother of two in her late twenties, she became a public-school teacher. As of the release of this book, she was finally able to resign from teaching to write full time!

Writing became a passion project, and she put out her first novel in 2021, and has continued to publish new novels every few months since then, not slowing down for even a minute. Married to a retired military officer, she spent many years moving around for his career, but they now live in central Alabama, with her youngest daughter, Arianna. Her oldest daughter, Brianna, is enjoying her happily ever after with her new husband and several pups. C. A. Varian has two Shih Tzus that she considers her children. Boy, Charlie, and girl, Luna, are their mommy's shadows. She also has three cats named Ramses, Simba, and Cookie.

www.ingramcontent.com/pod-product-compliance
Lightning Source LLC
LaVergne TN
LVHW011946070526
838202LV00054B/4822